This book belongs to

_____

Lola the
Lollipop Fairy

Lola's Big Top Bother

Other books in the series:

Good-bye, Moon, See You Soon

Lola's Lollipopper Showstopper

Lola's Lollipop Shop

Copyright © 2014 make believe ideas ltd
The Wilderness, Berkhamsted, Hertfordshire, HP4 2AZ, UK.
501 Nelson Place, P.O. Box 141000, Nashville, TN 37214-1000, USA.

www.makebelieveideas.com

Reading together

This book is designed to be fun for children who are just starting to read on their own. They will enjoy and benefit from some time discussing the story with an adult. Encourage them to pause and talk about what is happening in the pictures. Help them to spot familiar words and sound out the letters in harder words. Look at the following ways you can help your child take those first steps in reading:

Explore the story

Make the most of each page by talking about the pictures and spotting key words. Encourage your child to sound out the letters in any words he or she does not know. Look at the common "key" words listed at the back of the book and see which of them your child can find on each page.

Test understanding

It is one thing to understand one word at a time, but it is important to make sure your child can understand the story as a whole!

Ask your child questions as you read the story, for example:

- Do you like the big top?
- What trick does Lulu perform?
- What happens when Linda lifts her weights?
- Play "find the obvious mistake." Read the text as your child looks at the words with you, but make an obvious mistake to see if he or she catches it. Ask your child to correct you and provide the right word.

Activity section

A "Ready to tell" section at the end of the book encourages children to remember what happened in the story and then retell it. A picture dictionary page helps children to increase their vocabulary, and a useful word page reinforces their knowledge of the most common words. There is also a practical activity inspired by the story and a "Lola and her friends" section where children can learn about all of Lola the Lollipop Fairy's friends!

Lola, Linda, and Lulu are excited about the circus show tonight!

The fairies are practicing
in the big top. The big top
is old and full of holes.

Linda lifts her weights.
It starts to rain. Linda
gets wet!

Lulu spins her plates.
The wind blows
through the roof.

The wind blows the plates off the poles!

Lola juggles lollipops, but they fly through the roof!

The fairies need
a new big top.

Lola has a great idea.
Lola, Linda, and Lulu
get ready for a very
special show.

The special show is very exciting. Lola flies to the moon!

Lots of fairies come to see the new show. Now the fairies can buy a beautiful, new big top!

CIRCUS
SHOW

Ready to tell

Can you remember what happened in the story? Look at each picture and try retelling the story.

1

2

3

4

5

6

7

8

23

Lola's fairy dictionary

big top

wind

rain

weights

plate

juggle

Lola's useful words

Here are some key words used in context. Make simple sentences for the other words in the border.

The big top **is** old.

The fairies practice **for** their show.

The wind blows the plates **away**.

Lola has **an** idea.

The fairies get a new **big** top.

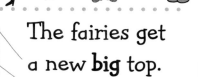

an · see · are · the · of · we · this · me · like · going · big · she · and · they · my

Lola and her friends

Lola is in charge of the circus show. Lola likes to think of new ideas, such as her lollipop shop! Linda and Lulu are her sisters.

Linda performs in the circus show with Lulu and Lola. Linda is a weight lifter. She also likes to sing and dance!

Lulu spins plates
in the circus show.
Sometimes she
juggles lollipops too!

Jaffa is the circus
cat. He likes to join
in with the shows.
Sometimes he wears
a hat, just like Lola.

Morris the mouse is
Jaffa's best friend. He is
very nosy! Morris likes
to know what is going
on at all times.

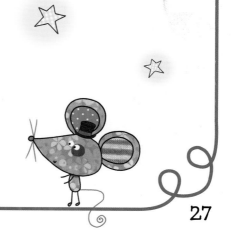

Lisa is Lola's friend and she loves lollipops! Sometimes she performs exciting tricks in Lola's circus show.

Lara is Linda's friend. She performs on the flying trapeze at Lola's circus. She is very good at it!

Lily is Lisa's sister.
She loves lollipops too!
Lily's favorite lollipop
flavor is lemon.

Lexi, Lulu's friend,
loves the circus show.
She likes Lola's cannon
ride the best, and would
really like to have a go!

Circus lantern

Make a lantern for the lollipop
fairies' big top!

You will need:

- 2 sheets of colored
  or patterned A4 paper
- scissors
- double-sided sticky
  tape or glue
- pens, glitter, and
  sparkly decorations

What to do:

1. Decorate one side of one of your pieces of paper.

2. Fold the sheet in half lengthways. Make regular cuts over the fold, making sure they finish about 1 in (3cm) away from the edge.

3. Unfold the paper and fix the ends together with glue or sticky tape to make a cylinder.

4. Cut a strip from the second sheet of paper and attach each end of the strip to the top of the lantern to make a handle.